Daddy Goes to Work

by Jabari Asim

Illustrated by Aaron Boyd

LITTLE, BROWN AND COMPANY

New York Boston

Little, Brown and Company

Time Warner Book Group
1271 Avenue of the Americas, New York, NY 10020
Visit our Web site at www.lb-kids.com

First Edition: May 2006

Library of Congress Cataloging-in-Publication Data

Asim, Jabari.
Daddy goes to work / Jabari Asim ; illustrated by Aaron Boyd.— 1st ed.
p. cm.
Summary: A young girl accompanies her father to his office, helping him throughout the day.
ISBN 0-316-73575-2
[1. Fathers and daughters—Fiction. 2. Offices—Fiction. 3. Stories in rhyme.] I. Boyd, Aaron, 1971- ill. II. Title.
PZ8.3.A777 2006
[E]—dc22

2004026621

10 9 8 7 6 5 4 3 2 1

Book design by Saho Fujii

TWP

Printed in Singapore

The illustrations for this book were done in watercolor on 110-lb. cold press rag board by Crescent.
The text was set in Claude Sans, and the display type is Andy-Bold.

To Nia, Jelani and Gyasi

—J.A.

For Dad and Abuela, who gave me a love of art

—A.B.

Brringggg! The alarm clock sings.
Daddy wakes with a sigh.
Slowly he rolls over
And opens a sleepy eye.

There he finds me
Standing by with a grin.
"It's seven o'clock," I say.
"Should we be heading in?"

I know it's very early
But there's lots of work to do.
Daddy's going to his office
And I'm going too!

Mommy helps me dress.
Daddy makes French toast.
Of all the breakfasts Daddy makes,
I like this one the most.

POLICE

Soon we're on the subway.
People are everywhere.
I read the funnies to Daddy.
Next stop, we'll be there!

We walk past shops and stores
And a tall man playing a horn.
Daddy likes to linger and listen
To the melodies being born.

Into the lobby we go
For an elevator ride.
My tummy feels all funny
As silently we glide.

Daddy shows his ID badge
To the guard on the fourth floor.
He pushes a shiny button
To let us through the door.

He smiles at me and says,
"Who do we have here?
I tell you, the workers
Are getting younger every year."

ABC
DESIGN

The people at Daddy's job
Are not surprised I came.
They smile and shake my hand
And already know my name.

Daddy laughs and jokes
As down the hall we go.
"We have a new boss," he says.
"Today my daughter runs the show."

Daddy's desk sits in the corner.
It's a very tidy space
With a computer, stacks of paper,
And purple flowers in a vase.

Hanging on the wall
Is a picture that I drew
Of Mommy, Daddy, and me,
And Little Brother too.

First we write a memo
To a client overseas.
I spell out the letters
While Daddy taps the keys.

Daddy's chair is noisy.
I hear its squeaky wheels
While he talks on the phone
About contracts and deals.

アロン・ボイド
RED HOT'S
ZIP

The morning passes quickly
When work gets done just right.
At noon we go outside
For some sunshine and a bite.

With so many hungry people,
Downtown is fast and loud.
Daddy holds my hand
And guides me through the crowd.

We take a walk after lunch
And savor the fresh air.
We watch people feed the pigeons
Near the statue in the square.

Back at the office,
A meeting's about to start.
I help Daddy carry posters,
An easel, and a chart.

In the conference room,
Everyone smiles and laughs;
I point at the numbers
While Daddy explains the graphs.

35%
51%
ABC
ABC

I hold up the posters
While he talks of sales and maps.
When he thanks me for helping,
Everyone else claps.

Soon it's five o'clock,
The end of our long day.
Daddy lets me phone Mom
To tell her we're on our way.

"You were great today," says Daddy.
"I hope that you had fun."
I'm so proud of Daddy
And all the work we've done.